Playing It Safe

A Kid's Guide to Staying Healthy, Happy, and Secure

Written by J.S. Jackson
Illustrated by R.W. Alley

ONE
CARING
PLACE

Abbey Press
St. Meinrad, IN 47577

I would like to dedicate this book and give thanks to all the good people and friends at Abbey Press who have given me the opportunity to contribute to this wonderful series of Elf-help Books for Kids. I would also like to thank my good friend, Bob Alley, whose wonderful artwork seems to get even better with each new book. It has been a great honor.

Text © 2008 J.S. Jackson
Illustrations © 2008 Saint Meinrad Archabbey
Published by One Caring Place
Abbey Press
St. Meinrad, Indiana 47577

Library of Congress Catalog Number
2008930644

ISBN 978-0-87029-416-7

Printed in the United States of America

A Message to Parents, Teachers, and Other Caring Adults

When we were children we lived in simpler times. We learned how to play safely at school playgrounds and how to steer clear of bullies. We were given boundaries in our neighborhoods and times when we were expected to be home. We learned how to make good choices—in our friends and in our activities.

Although children today are, generally speaking, safe and secure, they are forced to grow up faster and sooner. In today's economy, most parents work full time. Children who are home unsupervised after school require special safety measures. Preventing access to alcohol, tobacco, prescription drugs, and firearms is essential, and the family must agree on strict rules about after-school visitors, phone calls, and Internet activity. As older children gain independence, they need to learn the importance of making good choices and the concept of "safety in numbers." Whether walking home from school, hanging out at the mall, or riding bikes on the weekends, the "buddy system" can help kids avoid danger. While it may seem indulgent to some parents, providing children with cell phones does offer peace of mind and helps keep adults "in the loop" when children are out and about.

There is a glut of content inappropriate for children on television and the Internet today. Close monitoring, including parental blocking software, helps children make safe choices. Keeping home computers and televisions in "common areas," such as dens, kitchens, and living rooms, also helps in monitoring what children are seeing and hearing. Warnings about unsolicited e-mail and chat room communications are part of the protocol.

But as the times change, some things never do. There will always be a need for family togetherness, and love and support from parents. Try never to be "too busy" to listen when your child tells you about his or her day. Have meals together whenever possible. Always keep the channels of communication open. Remember, the closer we stay to our children, the closer our children will stay to us. And the safer they'll be.

—*J.S. Jackson*

Playing It Safe

When you were younger, your parents helped you learn how to play safely in your house—in the bathtub, on the stairs, in the kitchen. They also taught you how to play safely in your yard, your neighborhood, and at playgrounds. But while they were teaching you, they were usually right there with you.

Now that you're getting older, your parents will trust you to stay safe on your own. You have to remember what they've taught you and to make smart choices, whether you're out playing with friends or at home using a computer or watching TV.

Around Your Home

The two rooms in our houses where people get hurt the most are the bathroom and the kitchen. In the bathroom, of course, the tub can get real slippery with soapy water in it. If yours is slippery, you can ask a parent to get a rubber bath mat or some of those decals that stick to the bottom.

In bathrooms, electric appliances should always be unplugged when not being used. In kitchens, knives should be kept out of reach and never played with. When you're a certain age, an adult may choose to show you how to use them, and how to use the stove safely. Follow your parents' cooking rules.

As for stairs, always remember the saying, "Upstairs, no care. Downstairs, beware." If you fall going upstairs, you can catch yourself on the next step. Downstairs there is nothing to grab onto. Ouch!

In The Neighborhood

As you get older, you will be allowed more freedom in your neighborhood. Your parents will tell you where you can go and when you need to be home. Always follow these rules because there are times when things happen and parents have to find their kids right away.

It is always safer—and more fun!—to find a friend or two to play with. Look for fun places like playgrounds and parks. Try to stay near a house where there is an adult at home, so you can run there in case of emergency. And respect other people's property.

At School

Most schools provide enough teachers and helpers to keep you safe from harm. But you can still have problems with other kids on the school bus, on the playground, and in the halls.

These problems include things like teasing and bullying. Some kids just need to feel better about themselves, and that's the unkind way they choose to do it. The best way to deal with this is to ignore it and don't let them think they're getting to you.

If they keep on doing it, stay calm and say, "I don't like what you're doing, and I want you to stop." If they don't stop, say it again and again till they stop.

Malls, Stores, and Restaurants

As you get older, you will be given more freedom and responsibility. In shopping malls and stores, especially big grocery stores and discount chains, it's easy to get lost. Even grown-ups do it!

When your parents let you go on your own, make sure you remember where and when they say you're supposed to meet up with them. If things don't go as planned, get in touch with any store employee, usually by the cash registers, and ask them to page your parent.

But remember: It's best never to talk to strangers who aren't wearing a name tag or a uniform. If something scares you, go quickly to the cashiers and tell them.

Safety in Numbers

"Safety in numbers" is a rule even adults use when they travel to new cities and places. It's always safer to have a friend or two or three around when you're doing stuff, and it's always more fun!

Whenever groups of kids go places together— to the zoo, to the beach, on a hike—they are almost always asked to use the "buddy system." This system is a good idea no matter where you go or what you do.

Here are some good times to use the buddy system: riding the school bus, playing in your neighborhoods or the school playground, going shopping or to the movies.

"Home Alone" Kids

In many families, both parents work outside the home. After you reach a certain age, you may be trusted to get yourself home from school and into your home by yourself until a parent arrives. This is a very big step in your life and a great honor that you are trusted so much.

Because you are the "person in charge" of the house, it is very important to follow the "home alone" rules your parents give you. They may want you to call them when you get home. They may want you to get your homework done. They may have a chore for you. This is a very special privilege and it takes a very special person to do it.

Doorbells and Phones

Answering doorbells and telephones can be tricky if you're in a "home alone" situation. The first thing you should do is always make sure the doors are locked. It's also a good idea to keep a cordless phone or a cell phone handy with a "safety number" for quick calling. This is usually either a parent or a close-by neighbor.

When the doorbell rings, chances are it's either a friend or someone you know from the neighborhood. If it's a stranger, it's probably safer not to answer the door at all. If they keep knocking and won't go away, call your "safety number."

If you have an answering machine, you should screen calls. If it's a stranger, just let it ring. If you can't screen calls and a stranger asks to talk to a parent, tell them they're busy and can't come to the phone. Then offer to take a message. If they just hang up, you may want to call your "safety number."

The Internet and TV

Whether you are in a "home alone" situation or not, your parents should be able to trust you not to watch TV shows or go to Internet sites that they would feel you shouldn't.

If you have cable or satellite TV, even some of the daytime shows and movies are "R-rated." Ask yourself, "Is this something I would feel OK watching with my parents?"

The Internet puts so much knowledge at our fingertips. But it also has been the source of much trouble for kids and adults. Make sure to follow the guidelines set down by your parents.

Good Touching, Bad Touching

There's nothing better than a great big hug from a mom or a dad, or an aunt or uncle or grandma or grandpa. On sports teams and school playgrounds you see kids giving each other "high fives" and pats on the back all the time. That's "good touching."

There are other kinds of touching that feel wrong and shouldn't be done. That's "bad touching." But how can you tell the difference?

You may have heard teachers and parents talking about "the bathing suit rule." Pretend you have your bathing suit on. The idea is that no one should touch you in a place that the bathing suit covers. And remember, accidental touching—touching that happens only once and not on purpose—happens all the time and really can't be considered "bad touching."

God's Silent Alarm

We are very lucky because God gives each and every one of us something very wonderful. It is the deep-down ability to know right from wrong, good from bad. It is what we might call "God's Silent Alarm." It is that feeling you have or that voice you hear inside you that says, "this is wrong" or "this is dangerous." Some people call it "conscience." But it is just God's special way of helping you do the right thing.

Examples of when you might hear 'God's Silent Alarm" could be: 1. If someone dares you to climb a very high tree; 2. If a friend asks you to copy your homework; 3. If the doorbell rings and someone you've never seen before asks if your mother is home; 4. If someone touches you in your "bathing suit" area over and over.

Always Tell

Whenever you hear God's Silent Alarm, you know that something may happen to hurt you, your friends or your family. It is important to tell an adult that you trust whenever you hear that alarm. This could be a teacher, a parent, a neighbor, a policeman. You need to find someone to tell what is happening and ask them for advice or help.

Remember that telling isn't "tattling." Tattling is usually some little thing kids in school do just to try to get other kids in trouble. Telling is something that kids—and grown-ups—do to prevent something bad from happening or keep someone from getting hurt.

Alcohol and Drugs

Kids at a very early age are warned about the dangers of alcohol, tobacco, and drugs. Drugs include any kind of pills or cold medicines or cough syrup from the drugstore. Sometime you may be at a friend's house when the parents aren't home. If you are ever invited to try any of these three things—alcohol, tobacco, or drugs—God's Silent Alarm should go off loud and clear.

If there happen to be three or more people present, there may be "peer pressure" to join in. But you must listen to God's Silent Alarm and stand your ground firmly. Say something like, "I don't do things I'm not supposed to do. If that changes, I'll let you know."

Play It Smart, Play It Safe.

There's an old saying that says, "Look before you leap." There's another that says, "Think before you act." These are short little sentences, but they are very good advice. This is a great way for you to help keep yourself safe.

"Look before you leap" tells you to see what you may be getting into. "Think before you act" is asking you to imagine what may happen if you do something.

God's Silent Alarm is God's way of helping to keep you safe. If people used these more, and acted on them, there would be a lot less trouble and pain in our lives. And a lot more happiness and love.

J.S. Jackson is a husband, dad, and writer living in Lenexa, Kansas. The former manager of Hallmark Cards' creative writing staff, he is now a free-lance writer and editor. He is author of other Elf-help Books for Kids, *Bye-Bye Bully!, Keeping Family First,* and *Shyness Isn't a Minus.*

R. W. Alley is the illustrator for the popular Abbey Press adult series of Elf-help books, as well as an illustrator and writer of children's books. He lives in Barrington, Rhode Island, with his wife, daughter, and son. See a wide variety of his works at: www.rwalley.com.